ISRAEL

 **Marshall Cavendish** Benchmark
New York

This edition first published in 2011 in
the United States of America by
Marshall Cavendish Benchmark.

Marshall Cavendish Benchmark
99 White Plains Road
Tarrytown, NY 10591
Website: www.marshallcavendish.us

© Marshall Cavendish International (Asia)
Pte Ltd 2011
Originated and designed by Marshall Cavendish
International (Asia) Pte Ltd
A member of Times Publishing Limited
Times Centre, 1 New Industrial Road
Singapore 536196

Written by: Don Foy
Edited by: Crystal Chan
Designed by: Lock Hong Liang/Steven Tan
Picture research: Thomas Khoo

Library of Congress Cataloging-in-Publication Data
Foy, Don.
Israel / by Don Foy.
p. cm. -- (Festivals of the world)
Includes bibliographical references and index.
Summary: "This book explores the exciting
culture and many festivals that are celebrated in
Israel"--Provided by publisher.
ISBN 978-1-60870-102-5
1. Festivals--Israel--Juvenile literature. 2. Israel--
Social life and customs--Juvenile literature. I. Title.
GT4886.I7F69 2011
394.2695694--dc22
2010000305
ISBN 978-1-60870-102-5

Printed in Malaysia

136542

Contents

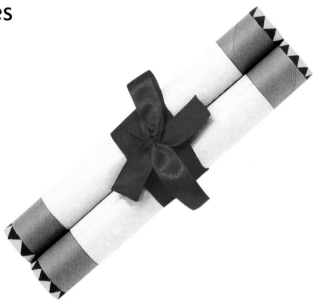

It's Festival Time . . .

Most Israeli festivals are a celebration of the Jewish faith. In Israel, festivals are usually based on a story, which reminds people what they are celebrating. Many of the stories come from the Bible and tell of things from the past. Some of the festivals are serious, while others are fun-filled and lively, with families and the community participating. Put on a Purim costume and join the party. It's festival time in Israel!

Where's Israel?

Israel is part of the region known as the Middle East, which lies between North Africa and Asia. It is a small country, only slightly larger than the state of New Jersey. Israel only became a country in 1948, but people have lived there for thousands of years. Many of the events in the Bible are believed to have taken place in the land now called Israel. The capital of Israel is Jerusalem. Jerusalem is a holy city for Christians, Muslims, and Jews.

Who Are the Israelis?

Most of the people living in Israel are Jewish. Many came to Israel from all over the world. Any Jewish person can become a citizen of Israel once they arrive in the country. People have come to Israel from countries that used to be part of the Soviet Union, such as Russia and Ukraine. During the famine in Ethiopia in the 1980s, thousands of Jewish people were helped by the Israeli government to settle in Israel. Even though these people have different backgrounds, they are united by their Jewish faith. Most of the other people living in Israel are Palestinians

✳ A young Israeli boy dressed for prayers.

4

and other Arabs, and they practice a religion called Islam. Throughout the rest of the Middle East, Islam is the most common religion. In Israel, however, Muslims are a **minority**. A small number of Christians also live in Israel. Christianity began in this part of the world many hundreds of years ago.

✳ The rock over which the Dome of the Rock was built is sacred to Jews and Muslims alike. This is where Abraham went to sacrifice his son Isaac, according to the Bible. It is also where Muhammad is said to have ascended to heaven.

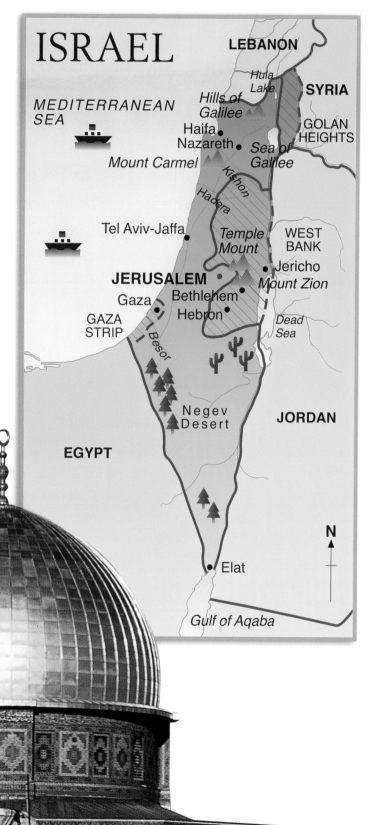

ISRAEL

LEBANON

SYRIA

Hula Lake

Hills of Galilee

GOLAN HEIGHTS

MEDITERRANEAN SEA

Haifa

Nazareth

Sea of Galilee

Mount Carmel

Kishon

Hadera

Tel Aviv-Jaffa

Temple Mount

WEST BANK

Jericho

Mount Zion

JERUSALEM

Gaza

Bethlehem

Hebron

Dead Sea

GAZA STRIP

Besor

Negev Desert

JORDAN

EGYPT

N

Elat

Gulf of Aqaba

What Are the Festivals?

In biblical times, people used a calendar based on the moon, called the lunar calendar. This is different from the calendar most of the world uses, which is based on the Sun and is called the solar or Gregorian calendar. Although the Gregorian calendar is used for everyday life in Israel, important dates, such as holidays and festivals, use the lunar calendar. This means that the dates of holidays and festivals in Israel change each year.

SPRING

Purim is a time to dress up and celebrate!

* **Tu B'Shevat** (New Year of the Trees)—This holiday is celebrated by planting trees and eating fruits.

* **Pesach** (Passover)—On this day, Jews tell the story of Pesach and families participate in a Seder, a ritual that includes a special meal.

* **Good Friday**—The Friday before Easter Sunday. In Jerusalem, church bells ring, calling people to remember Jesus Christ, the founder of Christianity.

* **Easter**—Celebrates the return to life of Jesus. Hundreds of people walk the route Jesus walked the day he was crucified.

* **Holocaust Memorial Day**—A day of commemoration for the approximately six million Jews who perished during the Holocaust.

* **Purim** (Feast of Esther)—The joyful celebration of Queen Esther's courage in helping to save her people.

* **Memorial Day**—A day in which to remember the people who died in the wars for Israeli independence.

* **Independence Day**—Celebrating the country's independence with carnivals, parades, and a fireworks display in the evening.

SUMMER

* **Shavuot**—This holiday celebrates the Ten Commandments, biblical laws followed by Jews. People also decorate the synagogue to celebrate the grain harvest.

AUTUMN

* **Rosh Hashanah** (Jewish New Year)—Jewish families gather for a feast on the first night of this festival. On the second night, fruits are eaten and a special blessing is said.

* **Yom Kippur** (Day of Atonement)—A sacred holy day in which Jews fast to make amends for their sins.

* **Sukkot**—A thanksgiving festival for the harvest when sukkahs, small shelters, are built and decorated.

* **Shemini Atzeret**—The day when Israelis say a prayer for rain.

* **Simchat Torah** (Rejoicing of the Law)—A celebration of the Torah, Jews sing and dance in the synagogues on this day.

WINTER

* **Hanukkah** (Festival of Lights)—This festival spans eight nights, during which Jews light a candle on each night.

* **Christmas**—Celebrates the birth of Jesus Christ.

MUSLIM HOLIDAYS

* **Mawlid an-Nabi** (Prophet Muhammad's Birthday)—This day is celebrated with festivities among the Muslims.

* **Id al-Fitr** (Feast of Breaking the Fast)—Muslims have a three-day feast to break the month-long fast of Ramadan. Some people dye their hands orange as a symbol of good luck.

* **Id al-Adha** (Feast of the Sacrifice)—Muslims honor Ishmael, the father of the Arab people, by sacrificing and roasting a sheep. After the feast, any extra food is given to the poor.

Pesach

Pesach, also known as Passover, is the oldest festival in Israel. It was first celebrated more than three thousand years ago! In every Jewish household, the family takes part in a ritual called the *Seder* [SAY-dur], in which someone tells the story of Pesach and a special dinner is served. Passover lasts for eight days.

The Passover Story

According to the Bible, a group of people called the Hebrews, or Israelites, moved to Egypt to look for better land and food. The Hebrews were a small group when they arrived in Egypt, but they were known as hard workers and admired for their wisdom.

Over time, the leader of Egypt, called the pharaoh, became worried that the Hebrews were becoming too influential and would turn against him. Over time, he made them slaves. The Jewish people were forced to make bricks to build Egyptian cities. They cried out to God for help, and finally their prayers were answered. Terrible **plagues** started to affect the Egyptians. Livestock died, boils broke out on the Egyptians' skin, and thousands of frogs covered the land. Finally, the pharaoh granted the Hebrews their freedom.

✳ The story of the Jews' escape from Egypt is called the **Haggadah**. On the first day of Pesach, parents tell their children the story so they will have a sense of what the slaves felt.

The Great Escape

When the Jews were escaping from Egypt, they did not have much time to pack and prepare food, such as bread. Bread takes a long time to rise and get fluffy. So the Jews made special bread instead. If the Jews had waited for the bread to rise, they might have been caught by the Egyptians. Instead they packed bread without any yeast, so it was flat and easy to carry. The bread is called *matzo* [mat-ZA], and it is what all Jews eat during Pesach. In fact, most bakeries are not open during Pesach because no one is allowed to eat leavened bread—bread with yeast—for the eight days of Passover.

✳ The pharaoh sent his army after the escaping Jews. The Bible says that when the Jews reached the Red Sea, God parted it for them to walk through. When the Egyptians tried to go through, however, the sea came together again and drowned them all.

✳ These two Israeli children are eating matzo, the flat, crispy bread that all Jews eat at Passover.

Burning the Hametz

The week before Pesach, the whole house is cleaned from top to bottom. This is to make sure that there is no yeast in the house. Sometimes little pieces of **hametz** [ha-METZ], as yeast is called in Hebrew, are left around the house, and it's the children's job to find them. The children go through the whole house with a candle and a feather to be sure it is clean. If they find any yeast, it has to be burned. The next day the family makes a big fire outside. They throw in all the yeast and burn it.

✳ A family of Jews gathers in the courtyard to burn the last of the hametz.

The Seder

The word *seder* means order. The food for the Seder meal is laid out in a special order to remind people of the escape from Egypt. This is a time for sharing. Many families invite students who are away from home or poor people to join them for Seder. After the leader breaks the bread, he says, "Let all who are hungry come and share this meal." Some people leave the door open during Seder so anyone who is hungry can come in and eat.

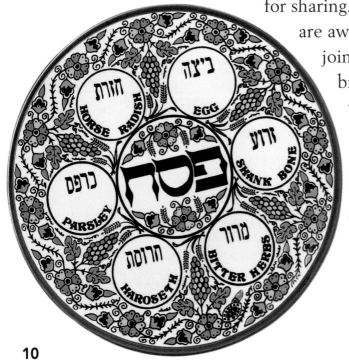

✳ This is a Seder plate. On the plate, there is a place for each one of the special foods that are eaten during the Seder to remind Jews of their struggle against slavery. There is also matzo, wine, and a bowl of salt water.

Hunting for the Afikoman

At the beginning of the meal, the leader of the Seder breaks one piece of matzo in two. Half is left on the table, and the other half, called the *afikoman* [a-fi-ko-MAN], is hidden. After the story of Pesach has been told, all the children go afikoman-hunting. The afikoman is very important because the Seder cannot be finished until everyone eats a piece of it. The child who finds it is very lucky because the Seder leader has to give a reward for the bread!

Did You Know?

The Jewish bible, the **Torah**, says that a father must tell his children the story of Pesach on the eve of the festival. Today family members also tell stories of more recent Jewish struggles against slavery. On Seder night, everyone leans on big, comfortable cushions. This is because slaves used to sit on hard stools without cushions.

✱ A family sits down to enjoy their Seder. Each one of the special foods is on the plate, including matzo.

Sukkot

Sukkot is one of Israel's harvest festivals. It takes place in the autumn. It's a time to give thanks for the food that has been grown and harvested in the summer months. Today the harvest is not as important as it was in ancient times, but Sukkot is still one of the most celebrated festivals in Israel and for Jews everywhere.

The Sukkot Story

As with many Jewish celebrations, there is a story behind Sukkot. As the story goes, after escaping from slavery in Egypt, the Jewish people wandered for forty years in the desert. To protect themselves from the harsh weather, they built huts to live in. These huts were called sukkot [su-KOT]—just one is called a **sukkah**—which is where the festival got its name. According to the Jewish holy book, every family must build a sukkah during the festival. If you are in Israel during Sukkot, you will see plenty of sukkot decorated with fruits and vegetables to celebrate the harvest. During Sukkot, people eat their meals in the sukkah, and some people even sleep there!

✳ According to the Torah, the sukkah must be no higher than 30 feet (9 meters), have at least three walls, and the roof must be made of leaves and straw. There must be enough open space in the roof for the stars to be seen.

✳ Opposite: These people are putting on a Sukkot play. They are dressed the way the Hebrews would have been after they escaped into the desert.

Lulav and Etrog

The *etrog* [et-ROG] and the *lulav* [lu-LAV] are symbols of the harvest. The etrog is a type of fruit, much like a lemon, from a tree called the citron. The lulav is made up of the branches of three different trees—the palm tree, the willow tree, and the myrtle tree. The branches are tied together and carried throughout the week-long Sukkot celebrations.

The seventh day of the festival is called Hoshana Rabbah. On this day, people celebrate by walking seven times around the synagogue, carrying the branches and fruit. As they parade around, they shout "Hoshana"—"God help us"—and this is why the day is called Hoshana Rabbah, which means Great Hoshana.

✳ This man is reading from the Torah while he walks around the synagogue on Hoshana Rabbah.

Shemini Atzeret

Sukkot lasts for seven days, but because another holiday falls right after it, Jews actually celebrate for eight days. The eighth day of Sukkot is called Atzeret or Shemini Atzeret, which means the eighth day of assembly. Shemini Atzeret is a holiday in which Israelis say a prayer for rain, called *geshem* [GE-shem]. Because Sukkot celebrates the harvest, people think a lot about the rain that helps the crops grow. In Israel, where the land is very dry, rain is a symbol of God's mercy. For the people who work and live on farms, the Sukkot festival is still a celebration of the harvest and the rain. In the cities, because people do not farm the land, the harvest is remembered and celebrated with the sukkah and the lulav and etrog. In this way, Jews, not only in Israel but all over the world, are linked together by their festivities and their religion.

✳ Everybody celebrates the Torah on Simchat Torah, and there is dancing and singing in the synagogues and on the streets.

Simchat Torah

Simchat Torah is actually the ninth day of Sukkot, but in Israel it is combined with Shemini Atzeret. Simchat Torah is a celebration of the Torah. Throughout the year, a part of the Torah is read on every Monday, Thursday, and each Sabbath. Jews begin reading the Torah in the synagogue on Simchat Torah and finish on the same day the following year.

Simchat Torah is the happiest holiday of all. On the eve of Simchat Torah, Jews sing and dance in the synagogues. They carry the Torah scrolls as they celebrate. The festivities in the synagogues often spill out into the streets. These street celebrations are called Hakafot parades. The Torah scrolls are carried at the front of the parade. The children follow, carrying flags and singing traditional Simchat Torah songs.

THINK ABOUT THIS

In some countries, the palm and citron do not grow, so they are imported from Israel. In these countries, a single lulav and etrog may serve a whole community. A child is chosen to look after them and take them around to every family on each day of Sukkot.

15

Hanukkah and Purim

There are two special events in history that Jews remember with festivals. Purim is the celebration of the deliverance of the Jewish people. Hanukkah, also known as the Festival of Lights, is the celebration of a victory in war. It is also the story of a miracle.

The Story of Hanukkah

More than two thousand years ago, there was a Greek king in Syria. He wanted everyone in Syria to worship **pagan** gods. The Jews, however, had their own faith, and they refused to give up their religion and their temple. A group of Jews led by Judah the Maccabee fought against the Syrians and won. When the battle was over, the Jewish soldiers went to the temple. They cleaned the temple and removed statues of the pagan gods. When they had finished, they went to light the lamp, but there was only enough oil for one day. They lit the lamp and celebrated until the lamp went out. Instead of burning for one day, the lamp kept on burning for eight days. That is why today Jews celebrate Hanukkah for eight days.

✳ On the eighth day of Hanukkah, all the candles on the menorah are lit. Each candle represents one day of the miracle of Hanukkah.

* Grandparents and grandchildren light the menorah together, which is the most important symbol of Hanukkah.

The Menorah

The **menorah** [me-no-RA] is the most important symbol of Hanukkah. A menorah is a candleholder that can hold a row of candles. It has always been a part of Jewish celebrations, especially the Festival of Lights. The Hanukkah menorah is different from the original menorahs in the temple. The temple menorah has seven branches to hold seven candles. The Hanukkah menorah has eight branches and a place for a ninth candle in the center. The center candle is called the *shammash* [sha-MASH], which means servant. This is because the ninth candle is used to light all the other candles.

Spinning the Dreidel

Dreidel [DRAY-dul] is a game played during Hanukkah. A dreidel is a spinning top with four sides. Each of the sides has a Hebrew letter on it. The players start by putting coins or nuts in the middle of a circle. Then they take turns spinning the top. As players spin the dreidel and a letter turns up, they take from or add to the goodies in the center. It's a fun way to pass the time while the candles in the menorah are burning.

* Each letter on the dreidel is an instruction.

17

Purim shpiels like this one are a common sight in the streets of Israel during Purim.

Purim

Usually the synagogue is a serious place, where people go to pray and pay their respects to God. During the festival of Purim, the atmosphere at the synagogue is very different. Purim is the celebration of a great Jewish woman's loyalty and courage in helping to save her people.

Esther's Story

According to the Old Testament, King Ahasuerus of Persia was married to a Jewish woman named Esther, who kept her religion a secret. The king's chief minister, Haman, tried to persuade the king to have all the Jews in the empire killed. Queen Esther's uncle, Mordecai, asked Esther to convince the king to save her people. When Esther went to the king and told him she was Jewish, he stopped Haman from killing the Jews by putting Haman and his followers to death instead.

Purim in the Synagogue

Because of the story of Esther, on the day of Purim, the people of Israel celebrate. Like other celebrations, there is a service in the synagogue. On Purim, however, people behave differently than they do normally. During the Purim services, the story of Esther is read aloud. Whenever the reader comes to the name of Haman, everyone drowns out his name with noisemakers called *gregers* [GRAY-gurs]. This erases the name of the man who tried to murder the Jews and helps people to forget him.

Gifts and Masquerades

Purim is a time of giving gifts to friends, family, and the poor. Looking after the poor or less fortunate is an important part of Purim. Large masquerade balls and parties are organized to help raise money for charities. At these balls, people dress up in disguises and masks. They dance and sing throughout the night.

Often a Purim *shpiel* [SHPIL], or play, telling the story of Esther is performed with costumes and music. All this fun is accompanied by lots of food and games, making it a favorite festival for all Israelis, especially children. At Purim, the streets are filled with children wearing costumes and playing. It is a little like Halloween, but without jack-o'-lanterns and trick-or-treating.

THINK ABOUT THIS

On Purim there was once a custom of choosing a Purim rabbi from among the schoolchildren of a town. This Purim rabbi would be a rabbi for one day and was allowed to make jokes about anything or anyone.

✳ Children celebrate Purim with costumes, plays, and lots of food and games.

Independence Day

At sundown on the eve of Independence Day, the mood of the country begins to change as people begin celebrating their independence. Families often go to the hills and light bonfires, sing songs, and tell stories until late at night. The next day, the real celebrations begin, with carnivals and parades all over the country. There is always a huge, colorful fireworks display in the evening.

In Israel on Independence Day, some children carry plastic hammers and gently strike each other on the head. As they hit each other, the children say "remember." This is to remind each other of the struggle the Israelis have faced to become an independent country.

Remembering the Holocaust

During World War II, millions of Jews were killed by Nazi German soldiers. This event is called the **Holocaust**. When the Jews living in Palestine heard about the things that were happening to the Jews in Europe, they began to fast and pray for them. The fast began on December 2, 1942. The people of Israel remember this terrible time in Jewish history every December 2.

✱ The Star of David is one of the symbols of Israel. It appears in the center of the Israeli flag.

✱ Opposite: Israelis gather to watch fireworks on Independence Day.

> **THINK ABOUT THIS**
> Jews believe that God promised them the land of Israel. This is why Israel is sometimes called "The Promised Land."

New Year of the Trees

Israel is in a very dry part of the world. It has few natural forests, and there is very little fresh water or rainfall. For this reason, trees, especially fruit trees, are very precious to the Israelis. Trees help to hold water in the ground and keep the soil from eroding. Tu B'Shevat is the new year or birthday of the trees—a time for celebrating the good things that trees bring and for planting new trees for future generations.

✻ One day of every school year is reserved for students to travel to the desert and plant saplings, or young trees.

Happy Birthday

The Hebrew month of Shevat, which is around February, is the beginning of spring in Israel. This is a time of new life, as the trees begin to blossom after the winter months. On the fifteenth of Shevat, the birthday of the trees is celebrated. In the Torah, there is a law that people must not eat the fruit of a tree in its first three years. In the tree's fourth year, the fruit is given to the priests. From the fifth year on, everyone may eat its fruit.

THINK ABOUT THIS

Do other countries have special days that celebrate trees? How important is it to preserve the trees we already have? What would happen if there were no more trees?

Weddings and Memories

It is an old custom to plant a tree on this day for each child born during the year. If the child is a boy, a cedar is planted. If the child is a girl, a cypress is planted. This way, the tree is always the same age as the child. In the past, when children grew up and got married, branches from their trees were woven together. The branches were used to hold up a canopy on their wedding day.

✳ Even though it's an old tradition, some young people are still married under a *chuppah* [hu-PA], a canopy held up by cedars and cypresses.

Today all kinds of trees are planted on the fifteenth of Shevat. Many trees are planted to remember those who have died. In 1949, the people of Israel began planting a forest of trees to remember the Jews who were killed during the Holocaust. Six million Jews are believed to have been killed. Today in Israel there is a forest of six million trees along the road into Jerusalem.

Things for You to Do

One of the best ways to celebrate any Israeli festival is by singing and dancing. Many of the Jewish festivals have their own special songs and dances. One of the most famous dances in Israel is a folk dance called the *hora* [ho-RA]. The hora is performed to any music with two beats per measure. There is a Sukkot song on the next page that is perfect for dancing the hora.

The Hora

1. Step to the left with your left foot.
2. Cross your right foot behind your left.
3. Step to the left with your left foot.
4. Hop on your left foot and swing your right foot across in front of your left foot.
5. Step in place with your right foot.
6. Hop on your right foot and swing your left foot across in front of your right foot.
7. Repeat this until the song is over.

When you have learned the steps yourself, teach some friends to dance the hora. Form a circle, and join hands or hold on to each other's elbows while you count out the steps. Once you have learned the Sukkot song, you can sing along as well.

Yom Tov Lanu

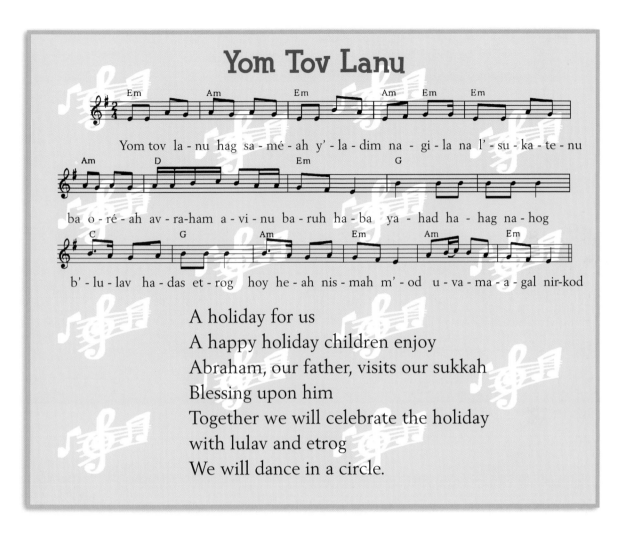

Yom tov la - nu hag sa - mé - ah y' - la - dim na - gi - la na l' - su - ka - te - nu

ba o - ré - ah av - ra - ham a - vi - nu ba - ruh ha - ba ya - had ha - hag na - hog

b' - lu - lav ha - das et - rog hoy he - ah nis - mah m' - od u - va - ma - a - gal nir-kod

A holiday for us
A happy holiday children enjoy
Abraham, our father, visits our sukkah
Blessing upon him
Together we will celebrate the holiday
with lulav and etrog
We will dance in a circle.

FURTHER INFORMATION

Books: *Harvest of Light (Hanukkah)*. Allison Ofanansky (Kar-Ben Publishing, 2008).

Israel: The People. Debbie Smith (Crabtree Publishing Company, 2007).

National Geographic Countries of the World: Israel. Emma Young (National Geographic Children's Books, 2008).

Sukkot Treasure Hunt. Allison Ofanansky (Kar-Ben Publishing, 2009).

Websites: http://www.israelemb.org/kids/index.html—Learn interesting facts about Israel and its people.

http://www.thejewishmuseum.org/kidzone—Explore Jewish holidays, play games, and make art.

Make a Megillah

A *megillah* [me-gi-LA] is a scroll. The Torah is made up of five different scrolls, or megillot. On the eve of Purim, the megillah that tells the story of Esther is read. You can make your own megillah by following these instructions.

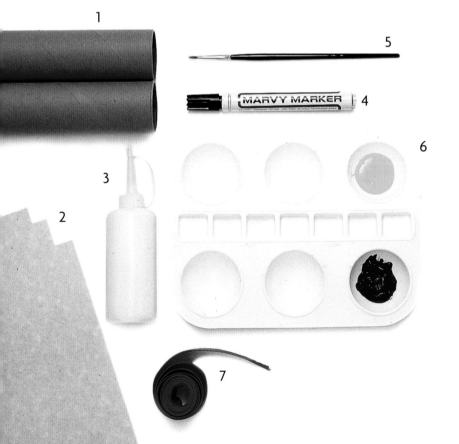

1 Write out the story of Esther in your own words on the paper. Use the paints or markers to illustrate your story.

2 Decorate the ends of the cardboard tubes with colorful patterns. You might like to use the star that appears on the Israeli flag, called the Star of David.

3 Glue each end of the paper to one of the cardboard tubes.

4 When the glue has dried, roll the paper onto the tubes.

5 Tie the scroll with the ribbon. Now you are ready to read your own megillah to your friends on Purim.

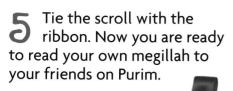

The Story of Esther

Many years ago King Ahasuerus married a Jewish girl named Esther. The King's minister didn't like Jews. He wanted to kill them all. But Esther convinced the King to save the Jews.

Make Hamantaschen

A favorite food served during Purim is *hamantaschen* [ha-MAN-ta-shn]. These are usually three-cornered cookies made with fillings, such as prunes or chocolate. Hamantaschen means "Haman's pockets." Enjoy making a version of hamantaschen with an adult helper.

You will need:

1. 1/2 cup (70 g) sifted flour
2. 2 teaspoons baking powder
3. 5/8 cup (125g) sugar
4. 5/8 cup (125g) butter
5. 3/4 cup (150g) chocolate chips
6. 2 eggs
7. 1 teaspoon vanilla
8. A wooden spoon
9. A spatula
10. A baking tray
11. A pot holder
12. Measuring cups
13. Measuring spoons

1 Wash your hands, and then mix the flour and baking powder together in a bowl.

2 Mash the butter into small pieces until the mixture is smooth.

3 Beat the eggs and add them and the vanilla to the flour mixture.

4 When the mixture is smooth, drop a small amount onto a greased baking tray and top with a few chocolate chips. You can also make the cookies into a triangle shape using your fingers. Keep on doing this until you've used all the mixture—about 24 cookies.

5 With an adult's help, bake the cookies in an oven at 350°F (180°C) for 15–20 minutes. Be careful around the hot oven—be sure to have an adult help you take the cookies out.

Glossary

etrog	A type of citrus fruit called a citron in English. It is carried during the harvest festival Sukkot.
gregers	Noisemakers used during Purim to drown out the name of Haman.
Haggadah	The story read at the dinner table during Pesach.
hametz	The ingredient in bread that makes it rise.
Holocaust	The killing of millions of Jews during World War II by the Nazis.
lulav	Branches from palm, willow, and myrtle trees.
matzo	A type of bread made without yeast and eaten during Pesach.
menorah	A special branched candleholder.
minority	A small group of people within a larger group.
pagan	Someone who worships many gods.
plagues	Disasters or very bad things.
Seder	The ritual and special meal for Pesach.
sukkah	Huts made from branches used during Sukkot.
Torah	The Jewish holy book.

Index

Photo Credits
Alamy/Photolibrary: 4, 9 (bottom), 11, 12, 16, 17 (top), 24; Corbis: cover, 1, 6, 7, 9 (top), 14, , 19, 21, 28; Getty Images: 10 (top), 15, 18, 22; Hulton Deutsch: 8; Itamar Greenberg: 13; Photolibray: 2, 25; Sybil Shapiro: 20; The Image Bank: 3 (top), 5, 10 (bottom), 17 (bottom), 23 (top)